NICK JR.
The
BACKYARDIGANS
Phonics Reading Program

Book 12
long *o*

Y0-CAW-158

# Stone of Power

by Sonia Sander

## SCHOLASTIC INC.
New York   Toronto   London   Auckland   Sydney
Mexico City   New Delhi   Hong Kong   Buenos Aires

"I am Yucky Man,"
said Pablo.
"And I am Dr. Shrinky,"
said Tyrone.
"We are going to get
the Stone of Power so
we can control the world,"
said Yucky Man.
"Wa-ha-ha-ha!"

"First we must get away
from those heroes.
If they catch us,
they won't let us go!"
said Dr. Shrinky.
"I will slow them down
with this goo,"
said Yucky Man.

"We will show you!"
said Uniqua.
"I am Weather Woman.
I will blow cold snow.
Now you are frozen!
Let's go, Captain Hammer.
We must get to that stone
first and protect it."

"I hope those bad guys
  are still frozen in the snow,"
  said Weather Woman.
"I know!" said
  Captain Hammer.
"I can build a boat to float
  across the moat so we
  can get to the stone."

"That boat will not help you when I shrink the moat," said Dr. Shrinky.

"Oh, no!" cried Captain Hammer. "Our boat cannot float, and those bad guys are running across the moat!"

"Throw the rope up to
the open window,"
said Dr. Shrinky.
"We don't have far
to go to get that stone."

"But we will get to the window first," said Weather Woman. "I can make the wind blow us there!"

"It's those heroes!" cried Yucky Man. "We've been foiled by them again!"

"The Stone of Power is
safe! Those bad guys
went home!"